Star of the Sea

A Day in the Life of a Starfish

Janet Halfmann

illustrated by Joan Paley

Christy Ottaviano Books

Henry Holt and Company ★ New York

Stars blink in the night sky above the rocky coast. Beneath the crashing waves, another kind of star clings to the rocks with hundreds of sticky tube feet. She is an ochre sea star, the common starfish of the Pacific Coast.

As the high tide rushes in, Sea Star crawls onto the shore to hunt. Water flows into an opening in her top and she pumps the water into her feet, making them work on the now-flooded land.

She inches along, twisting her flat body like a pretzel. Her mouth is on her underside, and she doesn't have a head or tail end. Tiny red eyespots at the tips of her rays tell her light from dark. She leads first with one ray, then another, heading for the mussels growing halfway up the shore.

All around her, the shore has come to life under the refreshing tide waters. Sea snails wander over the rocks and graze on algae. Sea anemones open like flowers. Crabs scoot out from cracks between the rocks.

Sea Star tries to grab a limpet for a snack. But the limpet quickly covers its shell with its slippery mantle. Sea Star can't get a grip.

She gives up and continues on her journey. Suddenly, a rock beneath her teeters, flipping her upside down. A fish swims over to nibble at her soft tube feet. But not for long.

Like a circus acrobat, she folds over two of her rays and grips the rocky shore with her sticky feet. She somersaults, landing right side up. The fish doesn't like her tough, spiny top and swims away.

Finally, Sea Star reaches the mussel bed. She hunches over a big mussel and grips its two shells with her strong feet. The tug-of-war is on! As she tries to pull open the shells, the mussel struggles to keep them closed.

But Sea Star won't get tired. Her many feet work like
a relay team, with some resting and others pulling.

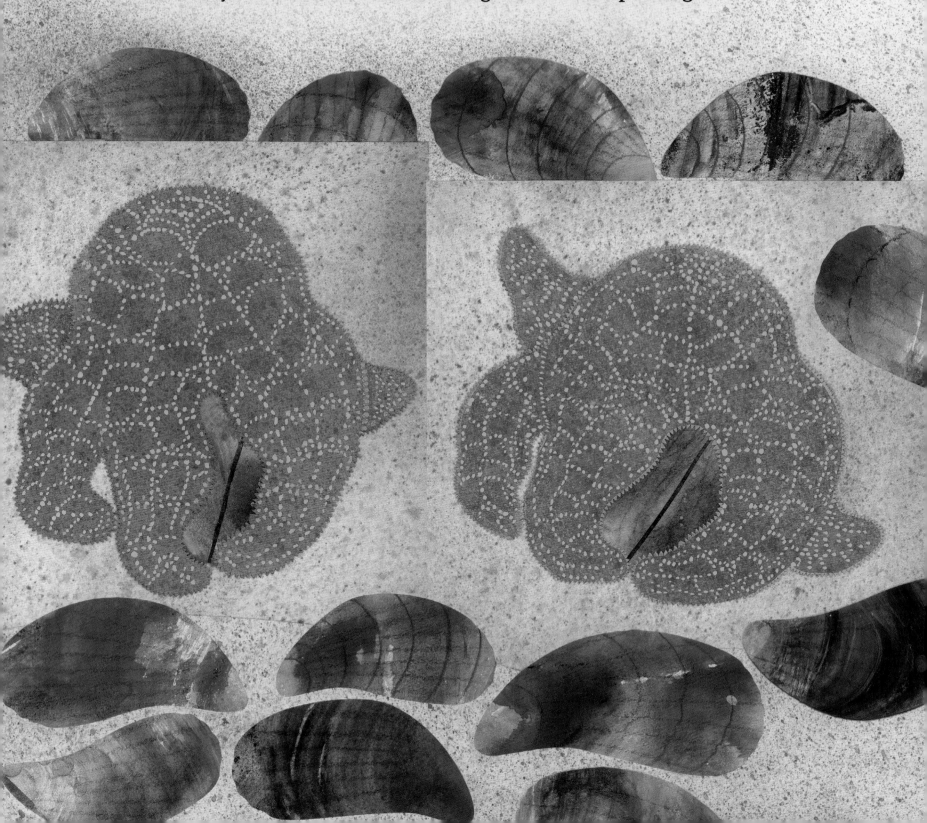

Soon the mussel's shells open just a crack. That's enough!
Sea Star extends her stomach right out of her mouth—and
into the tiny crack.

Slowly, her stomach turns the mussel's soft body to liquid,
right inside the shells. When Sea Star is done eating,
she pulls her stomach back in. Only
the shells of the mussel are left.

All night long, Sea Star feasts on mussels. When the tide starts to flow back to the sea in the morning, she is still eating. She finishes the last of her mussel, then heads down the shore toward the sea and home.

But she waited too long. The edge of the tide soon passes her by, leaving her uncovered on the shore. Without water, her tube feet will not work for long. As she feels for a crack where she can hide and stay moist, keen eyes spot her from above.

A seagull swoops down and snatches her. The hungry bird lifts Sea Star high into the sky by one ray, gripping her tighter and tighter . . . till—*chomp!*—the bird bites right through her ray.

Sea Star drops onto the seashore, startled but alive.
The seagull is left holding only a ray.
Quickly, Sea Star slides into a moist crack between
two rocks. She is safe.

In the afternoon when the waters of high tide
flow onto the shore once again, Sea Star completes
her return home. At the ocean's edge, she crawls
under some seaweed to rest.

With time, Sea Star's lost ray will grow back.
But for now, she will continue to hunt with four
rays—to the rhythm of the tides.

A Spiny Family

Sea stars often are called starfish. But the name sea stars fits them better because they live in the sea, look like stars, and are not fish. They don't have backbones or fins like fish, nor do they swim. Sea stars are echinoderms (*i-KY-nuh-durms*), or sea animals with spiny skin. Sea urchins, sand dollars, and sea cucumbers are all relatives of sea stars.

The ochre (*OH-ker*) sea star (scientific name *Pisaster ochraceus*) is one of about 2,000 species, or kinds, of sea stars. It may be golden-yellow to fit its name, but often is orange, purple, or brown. Other sea stars are red, green, blue, gray, even multi-colored. One kind looks like a star-shaped chocolate chip cookie!

Sea stars occupy ocean bottoms all over the world, from seashores to deep seas, in warm and icy waters. Their homes include tide pools, rocky shores, coral reefs, sand, and mud. Ochre sea stars live on rocky shores along the Pacific Coast from Alaska to Baja California.

Tube Feet and a Traveling Stomach

The typical sea star has five rays, or arms, but some have up to 50. The rays poke out from a central disk. The body bears short spines and often tiny pincers. The ochre sea star's spines sometimes form a star design. Nerves in the rays and elsewhere control the sea star's actions. There is no main nerve center (brain). Eyespots at the tips of the rays detect light and dark. Cells scattered over the body and tube feet sense light, touch, smell, and taste.

Sea stars crawl along on hundreds of tiny tube feet. In many species, the feet have sticky suction-cup tips for clinging tightly to rocks or prey. Water enters an opening at the top of the sea star and flows into a system of canals. The sea star squeezes the water into and out of its tube feet to move.

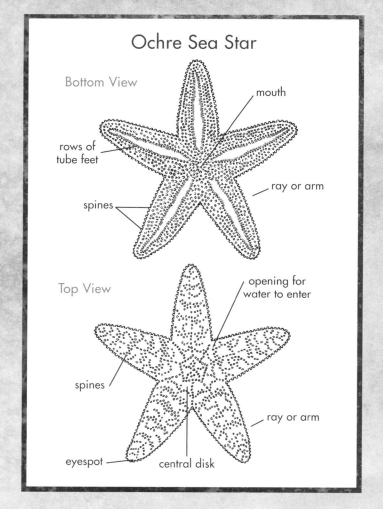

Ochre Sea Star

Bottom View — mouth, rows of tube feet, spines, ray or arm

Top View — opening for water to enter, spines, ray or arm, eyespot, central disk

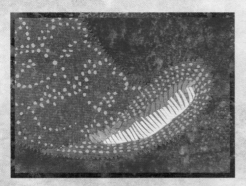

A close-up of Sea Star's tube feet

Many sea stars eat in a unique way—sending their own stomach out for food. This allows the sea star to devour prey too large to fit in the tiny, toothless mouth on its underside.

The ochre sea star ranges from six to fourteen inches wide. But some sea stars can fit on a dime, while others measure more than three feet across.

On the Prowl

Most sea stars are meat eaters, locating live or dead prey by smell and touch. A favorite food of the ochre sea star is the mussel. Because mussels tend to crowd out other animals and plants, the sea star is an important predator. It keeps mussels from taking over too much space.

Sea stars are fierce predators, causing panic as they prowl. Snails turn somersaults to escape, and scallops flap away. Besides mussels, the ochre sea star devours barnacles, snails, limpets, and chitons (*KY-tans*).

Few animals bother adult sea stars because of their tough, spiny skin. Occasional predators include gulls, sea otters, fish, and other sea stars. Many sea stars stay safe by wearing colors that match their surroundings.

A major enemy of sea stars is people, who often collect the animals for their bright colors. But the colors fade when sea stars die. Ochre sea stars can live twenty years.

Lost Ray? No Problem

Sea stars are experts at regrowing rays lost to rolling rocks or predators. In most species, a large part of the central disk must remain for the rays to grow back. Growing a new ray can take a year or more. Sea stars also regrow tube feet and other body parts.

About thirty species of sea stars use their ability to regrow body parts to reproduce. Some break in half to form a new animal. Others, such as the common comet star, can grow an entire animal from just one ray.

Swimming Babies

Most sea stars reproduce by releasing millions of eggs and sperm into the ocean in spring. Animals gobble up many of the eggs, but some unite with sperm and are fertilized. The fertilized eggs hatch into tiny swimming larvae that look nothing like their parents. For weeks, the babies swim and float—eating, growing, and changing.

Finally, they sink and attach themselves to the ocean bottom. There, similar to how caterpillars become butterflies, the larvae completely change shape to become sea stars. By the age of a year, the young sea stars are about four inches across and can have babies of their own.

Find Out More

★ Hirschmann, Kris. *Sea Stars*. San Diego: KidHaven Press/ Thomson Gale, 2003. [Lots of information about sea stars, with colorful photos.]

★ Monterey Bay Aquarium. "Sea Stars" in *Splash Zone: Rocky Shore Animals*. At www.montereybayaquarium.org/ efc/efc_splash/splash_animals_seastar.aspx. [Watch a video of a sea star's moving tube feet and oozing stomach.]

★ Sefton, Nancy. *A Coastal Journey*. The Poulsbo Marine Science Center, 2000. At www.poulsbomsc.org/coastal-journey/tutorial.htm. [Nancy and her marine biologist father explore the Pacific's rocky shore.]

★ ThinkQuest Junior. *Life on the Rocky Shore*, 2000. At http:// library.thinkquest.org/J001418/. [Award-winning student project featuring fun seashore activities, including a scavenger hunt.]

★ Zuchora-Walske, Christine. *Spiny Sea Stars*. Minneapolis, MN: Lerner Publications Co., 2001. [Easy text and large, colorful photos.]

Glossary

limpet (LIM-pit).   A mollusk with a low, cone-shaped shell.

mantle (MAN-tuhl).   Fleshy cape beneath the shell of a mollusk.

ochre (OH-ker).   A golden-yellow color.

sea anemone (uh-NE-muh-nee).   Column-shaped animal with tentacles around its mouth.

For everyone captivated by the wonder of sea stars,
especially my grandkids: Monae, East, West, Benji
—J. H.

To my family and dear friends, with love and gratefulness,
and a special wish for Sam
—J. P.

Henry Holt and Company, LLC
Publishers since 1866
175 Fifth Avenue
New York, New York 10010
mackids.com

Henry Holt® is a registered trademark of Henry Holt and Company, LLC.

Text copyright © 2011 by Janet Halfmann
Illustrations copyright © 2011 by Joan Paley
All rights reserved.
Distributed in Canada by H. B. Fenn and Company Ltd.

Library of Congress Cataloging-in-Publication Data
Halfmann, Janet.
Star of the sea : a day in the life of a starfish / by Janet Halfmann ; illustrated by Joan Paley.
p.   cm.
"Christy Ottaviano books."
Includes bibliographical references.
ISBN 978-0-8050-9073-4 (hardcover)
1. Starfishes—Juvenile literature. I. Paley, Joan.
II. Title.
QL384.A8H4 2011   593.9'3—dc22   2010024952

First Edition—2011
Designed by Véronique Lefèvre Sweet
The artist used hand-painted papers of watercolor blends and textures to create these collage illustrations.

Printed in January 2011 in China by South China Printing Company Ltd., Dongguan City, Guangdong Province, on acid-free paper. ∞

10 9 8 7 6 5 4 3 2 1